MEMORIES OF ANOTHER LIFE, ANOTHER TIME

Julie had lived her life at 912 Linton Street. But the things she was telling me now had nothing to do with Linton Street.

She dragged a sled up a snowy hill behind her house . . . but there was no hill on Linton Street.

She scratched patterns with her fingernails on frosty windowpanes that looked out on a brick courtyard that was not on Linton Street.

People came and went around her with the rustle of long skirts.

Pleasant memories of some childhood that the Julie Whitcomb *I* knew had never known.

But not all the memories were pleasant. . . .

On That Dark Night

Carol Beach York

BANTAM BOOKS

TORONTO · NEW YORK · LONDON · SYDNEY · AUCKLAND

RL 6, IL age 11 and up

ON THAT DARK NIGHT

A Bantam Book / October 1985

*Starfire and accompanying logo of a stylized star are trademarks
of Bantam Books, Inc.*

ISBN 0-553-25207-0

Published simultaneously in the United States and Canada

Bantam Books are published by Bantam Books, Inc. Its trademark, consisting of the
words ''Bantam Books'' and the portrayal of a rooster, is Registered in U.S. Patent
and Trademark Office and in other countries. Marca Registrada. Bantam Books,
Inc., 666 Fifth Avenue, New York, New York 10103.

PRINTED IN THE UNITED STATES OF AMERICA

O   0 9 8 7 6 5 4 3 2

On That
Dark Night

Chapter One

TERROR: *The silent scream in a nightmare.*

Yes, I think that's a good definition.

MURDER: *Something you think will never happen to you—but you could be wrong.*

I'm smart at definitions. They come easy to me.

THREE BLIND MICE: *A good place to begin this story.*

The last thing I expected to hear was "Three Blind Mice," but that's just what I heard as I ran up the porch steps of my girl friend Julie's house. It was

1

late August, one of those hot, drowsy days when you think time has stopped. Shadows seem to stand on the grass without moving, and although the calendar says it's still summer, you know in your heart that summer is over.

In the Whitcomb living room, someone was at the piano picking out "Three Blind Mice" with one finger.

When I reached the top step I stood on the porch, just listening for a few moments.

The living room windows were open, and the solitary notes, each one struck slowly and solemnly like a bell chiming, could be heard clearly.

> *Three blind mice*
> *Three blind mice*
> *See how they run*
> *See how they run*
> *They all ran after the farmer's wife*
> *She cut off their tails with the carving knife*
> *Did you ever see . . .*
> *As three blind mice.*

As soon as the tune was finished, it was started over. I listened a second time. Part of the ending was missing again.

> *They all ran after the farmer's wife*
> *She cut off their tails with the carving knife*
> *Did you ever see* (silence)
> *As three blind mice.*

I shifted my books and crossed the porch to the door. The inside door was open, but the screen door was latched. I peered into the gloom that always lies just beyond the screen on bright summer days.

"Julie! Hey, it's me."

The music stopped.

Almost at once I could see Julie coming into the hallway through the dusky indoor light to open the screen door for me.

"Hi, Allison."

"Last day!" I announced, flourishing my Spanish book and the Spanish-English dictionary with which I had struggled during the endless sessions of summer school classes. Mrs. Grimley, room 304. I think it was the hottest room in the whole high school.

"Oh . . . the last day." Julie seemed to be bringing her thoughts back from some place faraway.

She opened the screen door and I stepped into the hallway. It felt cool after the warm sunshine I had walked through all the way from school. I was counting on having a cold drink *immediately.*

"I heard you brushing up on 'Three Blind Mice,'" I said, putting my books down on the hall table. Next we would go back to the kitchen and get those cold drinks. . . . I turned around and saw that Julie had wandered aimlessly back through the archway into the living room.

"I said I heard you brushing up on 'Three Blind Mice.'" I followed her into the living room. "You've got that one finger pretty good. When do you start using the others?"

I was just kidding around, but she looked at me with such an anxious expression I felt guilty. "Come on, I'm only kidding," I said. "Play it with one finger, what the heck."

"I wasn't practicing." Julie shook her head and sort of drooped down on the piano bench.

"What's the matter?" I asked. Suddenly I felt uneasy. Obviously, something was wrong, but I couldn't think what it might be. It was just an ordinary summer day and I had come by my friend's house as I often did after Spanish class. Julie hadn't signed up for any summer school courses this year, and she was always glad to see me when I came by after Spanish. Sometimes we'd go swimming at the park pool; other times we'd go out to the mall and look at clothes or go to a movie. But today Julie seemed to be in another world. I knew she wasn't thinking about summer school or swimming or shopping. Something was wrong.

"Listen," she said, in answer to my question.

Julie sat down on the piano bench and played "Three Blind Mice" again.

The ending was missing some notes, just like before.

"Why is it like that?" Julie wasn't even looking at me as she asked the question. She didn't really expect an answer. "Why is that one part always missing?"

I had no idea, of course. Julie wasn't making any sense. And Julie was usually a sensible girl. She was my best friend. We rarely had any arguments or disagreements about things. She was shy around boys—and I was, too, at least around boys I particularly liked. But most of all, Julie was, well, *sensible*.

Julie began to play "Three Blind Mice" again, and I thought maybe I'd scream if she played it one more time! How did *I* know why some notes were missing? It seemed logical to me that if Julie would *play* the notes, they wouldn't be missing. But I guess that was too simple a solution.

"That's the way I always hear it in my head," Julie said, as she let her hands fall in her lap.

The room was silent. A car going by in the street sent a reflection of sunlight-on-chrome wavering across the living room wall. I wondered if anyone else was home. There didn't seem to be a sound in the house.

"You must think I'm crazy," Julie said apologetically. "It's just that . . . there have been so many things, Allison. 'Three Blind Mice' is just part of it."

"Part of *what*?"

Julie looked so truly unhappy that I thought she might burst into tears any minute.

She shook her head. "I don't think I can tell you. You wouldn't understand."

I was a little hurt. We were best friends. We had shared all kinds of secrets. We told each other *everything*. Why had Julie suddenly decided that she couldn't tell me something that I "wouldn't understand"?

"I'll understand," I promised rashly. "Honest I will, Julie. Just tell me what's wrong."

Whether I would understand or not, I was dying

of curiosity. Maybe I could pretend I understood, if it was something really weird.

Well, it *was* something really weird. At least most people would think it was weird.

WEIRD: *What people call things they don't personally understand.*

"All right, if you really want to know," Julie said.

Her voice had a note of hopelessness. She was sure I wouldn't understand.

"Sometime, a long time ago, I heard 'Three Blind Mice' played that way—with notes missing near the end. So that's the way I always hear it in my mind. I think I heard it played a lot, over and over, a long time ago."

"You mean when you were little?"

Julie shook her head. "That's the part that's hard to explain," she said.

Her face was partly turned away from me. She ran her finger slowly up and down the edge of wood below the piano keys.

"Do you know anything about reincarnation?"

I knew she didn't want a silly answer like, "You mean people coming back as cats or birds?" I wasn't sure what to say.

"Do you?" she repeated. She was very serious.

I thought about it. Then I said, "No, not much."

Which was true—except—

"I don't know much about it, either," Julie admitted before I could say anything more, "but I think I've lived before, before *now*. I was somebody else once."

She paused. The room was still.

"I think I've lived before, and I think I know *where* I lived."

She paused again, still sliding her finger along the polished wood of the piano.

"You're not laughing," she said, turning toward me slowly. "You're not laughing, Allison. You believe me?"

I wasn't laughing. I was fascinated by what Julie had said.

And I did believe her. Somehow I knew she was telling the truth.

Although what would come of the truth—and of my believing it—I couldn't begin to imagine.

Chapter Two

"Where do you think you lived?" I asked.

Julie continued to sit on the piano bench, and I sat down on the arm of a chair by the piano. I could see part of the front porch, and the flagstone walk that led to the sidewalk. It was just an ordinary summer day, like every other. Except not quite.

"Well . . ." Julie hesitated again. "Oh, Allison, I wish you really could understand."

"I *do* understand," I insisted. "Come on, tell me. Where did you live before?"

"I'm pretty sure it was in Greenbridge."

"Greenbridge?"

I couldn't keep the surprise out of my voice. Greenbridge was a small town about an hour's drive away. It was noted for historic old homes, antique shops, and quaint gift shops.

Julie smiled wanly. "You expected ancient Egypt or something like that, didn't you? Well, I probably lived way back then, too. I read this article once and it said you could have lots of different lives."

"Sure, I've heard that," I said. "But *Greenbridge*? So *close*?"

"Honest, Allison, I know it sounds crazy, but when I was there with my mom everything was so familiar and I was so afraid—"

"Afraid?" I interrupted. "Why were you afraid?"

"I don't know exactly," Julie said. "The town itself made me feel uneasy, and then there was something a woman in one of the shops said. Mom was looking for a certain kind of candlestick, and this woman said maybe Mom could find it in this other shop, and I didn't want to go there—I was just so *afraid*."

"Wait," I said. "Start from the beginning. When were you in Greenbridge? Was it your first time there?"

Julie nodded. "We'd never been before, neither Mom nor me. It was one day last winter, around the end of February. I remember the snow was melting and you could see patches of grass in the yards."

"You've had this feeling since way last February? And you never told me?"

"I never told anyone. And it wasn't just since last February. It's ever since I can remember."

"Ever since you can *remember*?"

Julie nodded. "You know how you remember things from when you were little? Sort of vague, half real? Well, it's like that. I remember things—odds and ends—but I know they're not from when I was a little girl. They're from a long time ago. I'll get this funny feeling and it's like there are other people around me, not the people I know now—oh, it's too hard to explain."

She was silent for a moment, and then she said, "Do you remember when I went to camp? I was about nine or ten."

I shook my head. "No, not exactly."

Julie and I hadn't been best friends when she was nine or ten.

"We used to sing songs around the campfire," Julie said, "and whenever we sang 'Three Blind Mice' I always felt funny—kind of strange and lost, like I should be somewhere else. And I knew that sometime, somewhere, part of 'Three Blind Mice' was missing."

She glanced up at me and then looked away quickly.

"Now you think I'm really crazy."

"No I don't," I said. "Honest, Julie."

We talked for a long time.

It was always easy for Julie and me to talk. Maybe that's how we got to be best friends in seventh grade.

BEST FRIEND: *Somebody you can really talk to.*

We'd known each other since kindergarten. I have all my class pictures from grade school, beginning with kindergarten, and Julie Whitcomb is in most of them.

There were pictures taken at classroom desks, all of us sitting with hands folded like angels.

There were pictures taken on the stage in the gym, with girls sitting in front in chairs and boys standing in back.

The teachers were always at the side, smiling.

Every year there was a picture, and it was fun to look back and see your friends grow up.

By the time our eighth-grade graduation picture was taken, Julie had changed from a front-teeth-missing little first-grader to a slender, pretty girl with hazel eyes and marvelous long lashes.

Everyone always asked Julie if her eyelashes were false, they were that long.

I had known her all that time. She had lived her life at 912 Linton Street. But the things she was telling me now had nothing to do with Linton Street.

She dragged a sled up a snowy hill behind her house . . . but there was no hill on Linton Street.

She scratched patterns with her fingernails on frosty windowpanes that looked out on a brick courtyard that was not on Linton Street.

She played in a barn one day, where pigeons cooed in a loft under the rafters.

People came and went around her with a rustle of long skirts.

Pleasant memories of some childhood that the Julie Whitcomb *I* knew, the Julie Whitcomb who had lived her life at 912 Linton Street, had never known.

But not all the memories were pleasant.

"I'd hide behind my mother's long skirts," Julie said, remembering.

"Why did you hide?"

"Because of Toddy," she replied; but when I asked her who Toddy was, she just shook her head.

Then she said her mother was cross and scolded Toddy . . . but no one scolded Toddy very much . . . because . . . well, she wasn't sure why.

It was confusing, and intriguing.

"Were you afraid of Toddy?" I asked.

"Oh, yes," Julie answered, as if I should have known this without asking. "We were all afraid of Toddy."

"We? Who's we?"

"All the little kids," she said.

The day she went with her mother to shop in Greenbridge had been a mild day for February. The snow was thawing. But Julie said she felt herself growing cold and uncomfortable as she went from shop to shop with her mother.

"Have you ever been to Greenbridge?" she asked me.

I shook my head.

"There are all kinds of shops. Expensive antique shops and little gift shops that aren't so expensive. We went into one of the gift shops, and all of a sudden I knew I'd been there before. I knew just what the stockroom in back looked like. I knew that beyond the stockroom were the rooms where the people who owned the store lived—a living room and a kitchen, and up a back stairway, the bedrooms.

"My mother was looking for a pair of brass candlesticks, just a certain size." Julie held her hands about ten inches apart. "All they had in the shop were those little glass cups you put candles in. So the woman who ran the shop said, 'Why don't you go over to Black Hill Road? There's a shop called Candlewick. They've got everything you could want in the way of candlesticks.'

"As soon as she said that, I got scared. I didn't want to go there. I thought something terrible would happen if we did. But Mom got interested in some other things in the shop, and I sort of hung around in the background, hoping she'd forget about going to that other place.

"There was a tea set on a pretty silver tray for sale. And suddenly I found myself thinking about Toddy, and how he put the spider in the teacup one time. I could see it plain as day, a big dead spider with hairy legs. Someone was just about to pour the tea . . . and one of the ladies screamed and then there was a lot of commotion. Everybody wanted to get away from the spider. But no one was allowed to scold Toddy."

I listened with a vague sense of foreboding, and I think I could almost feel the chill Julie had felt as she stood in the shop staring at a teacup and remembering another teacup and the dark body of a spider lying at the bottom.

"My head began to ache," Julie continued. "I

wanted to go home and lie down, and then I thought if I went through the shop and the storage room, and up the stairs by the kitchen I could be in my own bed and I could lie down and rest.

"I lived in Greenbridge, Allison—*sometime*. I know I did. And I lived in that store. My family owned it, I suppose.

"Anyway, it was awful. I felt the way you feel in the middle of a bad dream, scared and helpless. If you try to run away your legs won't move, that kind of dream."

"And if you open your mouth to scream, no sound comes out," I added. I knew the feeling, the terror of trying to scream, trying to run, and for a moment my thoughts were shattered by the echo of footsteps on a paved street, footsteps coming closer and closer . . . closer to *me*, in some vague dream I couldn't really remember. . . .

"What's the matter?" Julie was staring at me. "You looked like you were a million miles away."

"Oh, no, Julie, no," I assured her quickly. "I want to hear everything that happened. Really I do. Did you tell your mother you were afraid?"

Julie shook her head. "When I was little I used to try to tell my parents the things I remembered about—about another life. But she and Dad never understood. They said I shouldn't make up stories. No, I didn't say anything. I just wished I could go home and not have to go to that other shop."

Candlewick Shop on Black Hill Road. . . . I wondered what happened when Julie and her mother went there. To my disappointment, Julie said, "Mom lost track of the time in the gift shop. When she finally looked at her watch, she said she thought we ought to start home because it was getting dark and we had a long drive ahead of us. So—thank heaven— we never went to that other place."

Julie was so relieved about the way things had turned out, it seemed heartless to blurt out: "Oh, I wish you'd gone to Black Hill Road!" So I kept quiet, but secretly I wished things had worked out differently. I wished that as they'd come out of the gift shop into the darkening February afternoon, Julie's mother had said, "Oh, it won't take long, let's go take a look at the other shop anyway."

It would be growing colder as the sun dipped down, thin crusts of ice would be forming on the soft snow, and cars would turn on their headlights in the gathering darkness. How long a drive was it to Black Hill Road? Probably not far. Greenbridge was a small town. Maybe Black Hill Road was within walking distance.

"Allison—"

I was brought back from my imaginary visit to Black Hill Road by Julie's voice.

"Allison, when I remember things from that other life, I'm always a child. I don't think I ever grew up. I think something terrible happened to me in Greenbridge—and I never grew up."

Chapter Three

Julie made me a drawing of what she thought the back rooms of the shop in Greenbridge looked like. I wanted us to go to Greenbridge the very next day and see if somehow we could find out if Julie was right about the stockroom and the living quarters and the stairway by the kitchen.

"Maybe you'll remember some other things if you go back to Greenbridge," I suggested, but Julie didn't look very happy about that.

"I don't know if I want to remember other things," she said.

"But maybe we can find out what happened to you."

Julie shook her head. "I don't want to go back there again. I just wanted to talk to someone about it."

"Well, you have," I said. "You've talked to me. And I think you should definitely go back there and at least find out if the rooms behind the shop are the ones you remember. We'll go tomorrow."

I didn't see how anyone could resist going back to a place where she had lived another life. I couldn't. If I knew where I'd lived before, I'd be back in a flash.

FLASH: *Speed with which Allison Morley returns to scene of a former life.*

However, I didn't know where that was . . . at least not yet.

But Julie knew about Greenbridge, and we were going to go there.

I thought about it all the way home, walking along Linton Street, hugging my Spanish books.

How fast the summer had gone. Summer school was over; next week the fall term would start and Julie and I would be sophomores. I needed to get out to the mall and buy new jeans and sweaters. But now it was hard to think about anything except what Julie had just told me. All I wanted to do was go to Greenbridge. I had to decide what I would tell Mom. I couldn't come right out and say, "Julie and I want to go to Greenbridge tomorrow and find out some more about the life she used to live there a long time ago."

At the corner of Atlanta Street I turned right. From halfway down the block, I could see the forsythia bushes that grew along the side of our front yard. My little brother Jimmy's bike was lying abandoned in the middle of the lawn, and in the yard next to ours I saw him with a gang of kids, racing through a lawn sprinkler with shrieks of delight.

My thoughts had been so far away it was hard to come back to this everyday, summer-in-the-suburbs life. In my mind I could still hear gasps of surprise, a frightened scream, the sound of chairs pushing away from a table where a huge spider sprawled in a teacup. *Toddy did it!* someone cried. . . . *Mustn't scold Toddy.*

I walked past the abandoned bike and around to the back door. I found a note from Mom on the kitchen table: *I'm next door.*

I put down my school books, got a can of ginger ale out of the refrigerator—I never did get the cold drink at Julie's—and went upstairs to my room.

Next door meant Mom was at the Donahues'. While the neighborhood kids ran through the sprinkler in the Donahue yard, Mom and Mrs. Donahue would be sitting on the side porch having iced tea and chatting lazily.

I stood at my window, watching the kids play and drinking the ginger ale.

I decided I would tell Mom that Julie and I wanted to go to Greenbridge just for fun, to see the shops. Mom would understand that. She went to Greenbridge sometimes to look for antiques. In fact, Mom would not only understand, she would be all for it. She might even offer to come along, to drive us, so she could do some shopping herself.

And that wouldn't be so good.

I turned away from the window restlessly. Julie and I wanted to go alone. What would I say if Mom offered to drive us?

Then I remembered that the next afternoon Mom's book club would meet. Julie's mother would be at the meeting too. Both our mothers would be sitting in someone's living room listening to a book review and not giving a second thought to where Julie and I were.

And Julie and I would be in Greenbridge.

Everything worked out just as I'd thought it would. And at 12:10 we caught the bus at the corner of Crawford Avenue.

"What did your mom say?" I'd asked, as I met Julie at the bus stop. "Was she suspicious or anything?"

Julie adjusted her sunglasses. "No, she thinks it's a nice idea."

"My mom does, too," I said.

Once out of town, the bus sped along the highway, past fast-food places and car lots, past the Riverton Mall, and then into a stretch of countryside with only an occasional house.

The ride to Greenbridge was about an hour long, so Julie and I had plenty of time to talk. We huddled together in our seats and unfolded the pieces of paper that Julie had drawn on. There was the shop, a large square room. Directly behind the shop she had drawn the storeroom. Beyond the storeroom was a room Julie said was the living room and beyond that was the kitchen.

"There's a stairway here." Julie pointed to her drawing. "It leads from this hallway by the kitchen up to the bedrooms. And under the stairs there's a kind of cupboard where we kept coats and boots and things like that."

As we got closer to Greenbridge, I noticed farmhouses and barns. Julie had mentioned playing in a barn where there were pigeons in the loft. I wondered if Julie's long-ago family had known someone who lived on a farm near Greenbridge, and if she had visited there as a little girl and played in the barn. The countryside was hilly in places, too; maybe it was behind one of these farmhouses that she had pulled her sled on snowy days.

The bus station in Greenbridge was a small, weatherworn building with a wooden bench by the door. The bench had recently been painted a bright green, and on the back of the bench *Welcome to Greenbridge* had been painted in white.

Julie and I got off the bus and stood by the curb. Across the street from the station was a row of quaint shops, and I looked around with interest.

"Which shop were you in?" I asked Julie, as the bus rumbled away down the street.

"None of these." Julie followed my gaze to the shops across the street. "We have to go down to that corner, then you'll see it."

We walked slowly down the street, and as we turned the corner, we entered an old-fashioned town square paved with bricks, a fountain splashing water from the mouths of two stone fish, leafy maple trees shading benches. I stared with fascination. It was like going back years in time just to stand in that square.

Surrounding the square were the shops for which Greenbridge was known. People were coming and going between them. Greenbridge was a popular place; a large parking area nearby was well filled.

I wondered where Black Hill Road was and if I could talk Julie into going there, to Candlewick. When she'd agreed to come to Greenbridge she'd said she didn't want to go to Candlewick, but I thought maybe I could change her mind.

Julie nudged me and pointed toward a shop called Martha-Ann Gifts, tucked between a bakery and an antiques store.

"That's it," Julie said.

We walked toward the store, and I sensed adventure waiting behind the blue door. I glanced up just before we went inside and saw two small windows in the second story, framed by white ruffled curtains. Were those the windows Julie had looked out of once upon a time when she was some other girl, with another name? What had her name been then, when she lived here and all the children were afraid of Toddy?

Julie opened the shop door, and as we stepped inside, a bell jingled merrily. No one paid any attention to it, however. Several customers were in the shop and a plump, gray-haired woman stood behind a counter helping one of them.

"Is that the woman who told your mom to go to Black Hill Road?" I whispered to Julie.

Julie shook her head. She looked around the shop, and just then a woman came through a doorway at the back carrying a large cardboard box. "That's her," Julie said under her breath.

We watched as the woman began to unpack china salt and pepper shakers from the box and arranged them on a shelf.

I wanted to rush up to her and ask her to let Julie and me go back and see what was behind the door. But I couldn't do that. We didn't really have much of a plan as to how we could find out if the back rooms looked the way Julie thought they did. I had been sure I'd think of some clever way to do that, but I hadn't come up with a thing yet.

I looked around the shop. Every display table and shelf was overflowing. There were carved napkin rings, dried flower arrangements, small vases and figurines, notepaper, engagement books, fancy pot-holders, straw place mats, tile trivets, small brass animals and birds. If you needed a gift for someone, you could surely find it here.

The woman had finished unpacking the salt and pepper shakers, and Julie was actually going over to her. Julie's face was strained-looking—at least to me—but she spoke to the woman quite calmly.

"I used to know some people who lived here once," Julie said, taking a chance.

The woman smiled pleasantly. "Is that so?"

I breathed a sigh of relief.

The woman was silvery-haired but not as plump as the woman at the cash register. She wore a red smock over her dress, and a pair of comfortable-looking, flat-heeled shoes.

"We're new here, my sister and I." She nodded toward the woman who was ringing up a sale at the register. "This is our first year in Greenbridge. She's Martha, I'm Ann."

Julie looked uncertain as to what to say next, and she glanced at me nervously as I moved to her side. "Have you changed anything in the—in the house?"

Julie hadn't wanted to come back to Greenbridge, but now that she was here, the past was pulling at her again, making her want to know the things and see the things that had once been part of her life. She wanted to go into the rooms behind the shop so intensely I could hear it in her voice, in the tense, yearning way she asked if anything was changed.

"Not much. We might paint some next year. Kitchen could use it." The woman paused. For a moment a bemused expression crossed her face, as if the conversation seemed a bit unusual to her.

"Is the window seat still in the kitchen?" Julie pressed on.

"Oh, we won't make any structural changes." The woman looked surprised even to think of this. "No, the most we'll do is put on some fresh paint."

"Is the cupboard still under the stairs?"

I stood close to Julie, so the woman could see we were together. With a growing sense of excitement I listened as she kept assuring Julie that everything was just the same as it had always been, the cupboard under the stairs, the window seat in the kitchen, everything.

"But it isn't really the same," Julie said finally, with a note of sadness. "You've moved your own furniture in—it must all look so different."

"That may be," the woman conceded, "but we're very happy with the way our things fit in. Sometimes when you move, things don't fit the new place, but we were lucky." Then, impulsively, she added, "Maybe you'd like to see how it looks now, with our furniture."

I wanted to poke Julie and say, "Hey, how about this for luck!" but Julie seemed to have forgotten I was there. She was staring straight ahead with hypnotic intensity, and I knew the only voice she was listening to was the voice of the woman who was leading us along like a tour guide.

"This is the storeroom. Don't mind the mess, we've been getting in new merchandise and it's not very neat right now." She led us through a cluttered room behind the shop, exactly like the room Julie had drawn in her sketch.

"And this is our little home." The woman opened a door at the end of a small passageway behind the storeroom, and there was a room comfortably furnished with a sofa and chairs, a television set, and a piano.

"It's very nice," I said politely. Julie looked as

though she was in a trance. I was afraid the woman would notice, but she was busy talking.

"We've always wanted a little shop like this, and now that we're both widows we decided to just *do* it. Now, here's the kitchen—I should say Martha's kitchen. She's the Julia Child."

The kitchen and living room were exactly as Julie had drawn them. And the cupboard was under the stairs. It was full of empty flowerpots and gardening tools.

"We have a little garden in back," the woman explained as we looked into the cupboard. I think she was going to show us the garden, but Julie's attention was caught by a round pane of colored glass in the wall by the stairway landing. She was staring at it so intently that the woman's voice faded away. She looked at Julie uneasily. "Is something the matter?"

Julie didn't take her eyes from the small stained-glass window. She remained silent.

"Is something the matter?" the woman repeated. Her face wasn't quite as friendly now. Julie took a step or two closer to the stairway and put her hand on the banister. The woman looked startled, as though she was about to remind us that she hadn't invited us upstairs.

"On sunny mornings the light would shine through the little window," Julie said at last. "We could see all the pretty colors reflected on the carpet."

The woman looked taken aback. Her eyes narrowed and she stared at Julie suspiciously.

"How long ago did you say your friends lived here?"

Julie didn't answer. I don't think she even heard.

"It was a long time ago," I said, hovering apologetically in the background.

The woman looked at me, and then back at Julie. "I happen to know," she said severely, "that the building next door is nearly as old as this one, which was built in 1905. The other house was built about ten years later. And it was built so close that no sunlight ever comes through that colored window. It hasn't for decades."

"But I remember the window," Julie said softly. She turned to me. "I do remember it, Allison. And I remember the circle of colored light it made on the landing when the sunshine came through. It was so pretty."

There was an awkward silence. I knew the woman thought Julie was lying to her, for whatever reason. And it was occurring to her now that she had rashly brought two total strangers into her home and that something was very odd about the whole thing.

"I must get back to the shop," she said abruptly, and I knew she was anxious to have us *out*.

We followed her silently back through the kitchen, living room, and storeroom. Several customers were in the shop, and the woman's sister, Martha, was wrapping a package for one.

"Thank you," Julie said, like someone in a trance.

The woman didn't answer. I knew she just wanted us to go away.

"Well, good-bye," I said as cheerfully as I could.

The woman nodded vaguely at me and then looked again at Julie's pale face.

Julie started toward the shop door, and as she opened it to go out, I turned back for a last question.

"How far is Candlewick on Black Hill Road?"

"About half a mile," the woman answered coldly. "You go across the square and then on past the library."

I nodded and hurried after Julie. All I had to do now was talk her into going to Black Hill Road.

Chapter Four

Persuading Julie to go to the candle store on Black Hill Road wasn't easy. First we sat on a bench in the square by the fountain and talked about it, and she kept saying maybe we should just get a bus and go back home.

"Go back? We just got here," I said. "Besides, think of everything we've already found out. We might find out lots of other things if we go to Candlewick."

We crossed the square at last and walked along Black Hill Road, admiring the spacious old houses and the spreading willows and elms shading the yards. We passed the library with a flag flying from the flagpole on the lawn, and a few blocks later we came to the last house. It was almost hidden by lilac bushes the size of small trees. A flowery scent drifted to us from a row of smaller white-flowered bushes.

"What *is* that?" I asked Julie, taking deep breaths of the marvelous smell. "Maybe it's honeysuckle. Isn't it honeysuckle that's supposed to smell so good?"

Julie wasn't happy to be going to Candlewick, but she had to laugh when I said that. "How would *I* know? Honestly, Allison!"

Beyond the house with the lilac bushes and the white flowers, the street narrowed and became a bridge crossing a stream. We stood on the bridge and looked down into the gently flowing water.

"Come on," I said finally, "we're probably almost there." As we reached the other side of the bridge we could see a cluster of quaint, old-fashioned shops like the ones in the square. They were set back from the street in little cobbled courtyards.

We found Candlewick easily enough, and Julie didn't seem as nervous or frightened as I'd thought she would. As we opened the door and went inside, her first words were: "Oh, Allison, isn't this beautiful!"

The shop was dimly lighted. Along the shelves dozens of candles had been lit in small glass cups. Flickering spots of candlelight glowed through red, amber, blue, and green glass.

Behind the shelves, the walls were mirrored, and the glowing lights seemed to be lighting other rooms in the mirrors. The shop was like a fairyland.

There was nothing to be afraid of here. Julie looked puzzled and a little sheepish as she glanced at me and shrugged her shoulders.

Near the back of the shop a young salesman was waiting on a customer. Julie and I stayed near the door. "Are you getting any memories?" I asked, leaning close to her. Her face, lightly tanned at the end of the summer, looked darker in the dusky light of the candle shop.

"No, I'm not," she said, puzzled. "This place doesn't seem familiar at all. But there must be *something* about it, or why did I have that awful feeling when the woman told my mother to come here?"

"It looks a lot newer than those shops around the square," I said. "Maybe it wasn't even here when you lived in Greenbridge."

"Do you think so?" Julie looked doubtful. "It looked old on the outside."

"I think it was just made to look that way. Let's ask." The salesman had finished waiting on his customer, and he was smiling as he came toward us through the glowing candles.

"Can I help you young ladies?"

"We like your store," I said, nudging Julie.

She nodded and said, "Yes, it's beautiful."

"Thank you." The young man looked pleased. "Are you looking for anything in particular?"

"Oh, no," I answered, trying to sound as if I might buy something eventually. "We were wondering how old the store is."

"About ten years, I would say. It's my father's shop, so I should know exactly how old it is. It's either ten or eleven."

"Are you sure?" Julie asked with a confused

expression. A shop only ten years old had nothing to do with her life in Greenbridge long ago.

The young man folded his arms across his chest and lounged back against a display table of silver candlesticks and candle snuffers. "All of the shops here along Black Hill Road are newer than the shops around the square," he said pleasantly. "Some of those buildings are a hundred or even two hundred years old. But recently Greenbridge has become so popular that it's begun to expand. These new shops were built along Black Hill Road. Of course there were regulations set as to the type of buildings that could be put up. We had to keep in harmony with the old shops around the square. And we like people to think these really *are* old shops." He winked at us in a conspiratorial manner. "Most people don't ask."

I felt my face flush. "I'm sorry," I mumbled. "We just wondered."

The young man shrugged good-naturedly. "That's okay. We fool most of the people. But you can't fool all of the people all of the time, can you?"

Now that we *had* asked, the man seemed quite willing to talk about the shops on Black Hill Road.

"From what I've been told," he said, "years ago, nobody wanted to build shops—or homes—this side of the bridge. Too close to the cemetery. Kind of superstitious, I suppose. But now it doesn't seem to matter so much."

A woman with a little girl came in, and the young man straightened up. "You two make your-

selves at home," he said to us as he moved off to greet
the new customers. "Look around all you want to."

But there was nothing we wanted to buy, and as
the salesman and the woman went to the other end of
the shop, Julie and I slipped outside.

We stood uncertainly on the sidewalk by Candlewick, looking up Black Hill Road. The street curved
to the left about a block farther on. The shops
appeared to come to an end there, and large trees
blocked our view of what lay beyond.

"I wonder how far it is?" Julie said.

I knew she meant the cemetery. It had been the
cemetery that frightened her all along. It had been
the mention of Black Hill Road that scared her that
day in the shop, not the name of Candlewick.

"I bet when you lived here, you were scared of
the cemetery," I said. "All little kids are scared of
cemeteries. When you lived here, Black Hill Road
was probably only a deserted stretch of road, where
the graveyard was."

Julie looked down at the road. A light breeze
lifted strands of her soft brown hair.

"Sure, that's it," I said.

We began to walk on, and as we passed the trees
by the curve of the road, we saw Greenbridge
Cemetery behind a high black iron fence. The front
gate was open, and as we watched, a man and woman
walked out of the cemetery grounds to a car parked at
the side of the road. The woman was carrying
gardening gloves and a small wicker basket. I thought

they had probably been putting flowers by a grave somewhere behind the black iron fence.

As their car drove off, Julie and I walked closer and stood by the fence, looking through the bars into the cemetery. A few early-falling leaves fluttered down from the trees that stood along the winding paths. There were flowers beside some of the grave-stones; other graves looked forlorn and untended and forgotten.

Julie was deep in thought, and I stood beside her silently. I knew she would tell me if she remembered anything special.

"We came here once at night," Julie said at last. She drew herself close to the iron rails and stared into the cemetery. "A whole bunch of us kids came at night. Toddy said we couldn't do it, we'd be too scared. He dared us to come. So we all came, to show him we weren't afraid. But I was. I was afraid."

I looked at the cemetery basking in the sunlight. It looked harmless enough in broad daylight. But I didn't think I'd want to be in it after dark, after the gate was closed and only the dead people and their gravestones were left.

Julie turned away from the fence abruptly. "Come on, Allison. Let's go back to the bus."

"Toddy sounds pretty awful to me," I said as we started walking back the way we had come. "Daring little kids to go into a spooky place like a cemetery at night. Putting spiders in teacups."

"Yeah," said Julie. "And one time my mother opened our door and a big dead bird was lying on the doorstep—a crow or something. Black. *Big*. Its wings were spread out like it was going to fly right into the kitchen."

"Ugghhh!"

Julie looked down at the ground, watching her feet as we walked along. "My mother screamed, and I hid behind her skirts. I thought that bird was going to fly in and peck out my eyes."

"Julie! How awful! What made you think that?"

"I don't know exactly." Julie pushed at her sunglasses. "Maybe somebody told me birds would do that."

"Toddy, probably," I said grimly. "And he put the bird there by your door, didn't he?"

"Yes," Julie answered slowly. "But we couldn't scold him, not that summer."

"What do you mean, not that summer?"

"I don't know." Julie looked confused. "We used to scold Toddy—and then we weren't supposed to anymore."

It didn't make much sense to me, but Julie didn't seem to have anything more to say about it.

"Toddy liked dead things," I said. "Spiders and birds and cemeteries."

Julie nodded her head and gave a shudder.

We crossed the bridge then and walked back past the house with the lilac trees and honeysuckle bushes. Well, maybe honeysuckle. Julie's face was thoughtful, and she looked intently at the old houses we were passing.

"Do these houses look familiar?" I asked. I wanted Julie to remember everything she could.

"Not specifically. Not like the shop where I used to live. I do feel as if I've walked along this street before, like I'm not really in a strange place."

I looked around at the old houses. I thought I would like living in an old house with a big attic and gables and corner rooms with slanting roofs. And a side porch, with a porch swing suspended by chains. Was the room I sometimes saw in my mind, like a long-ago place almost forgotten, was that room in a house like the houses on Black Hill Road? I tried to feel something special for the houses, some stirring, but I didn't feel anything. Greenbridge was Julie's town, not mine.

As we crossed the square to go back to the bus station, Julie said, "Well, now you've seen Greenbridge."

Yes, now I had seen Greenbridge. Soon we would be on the bus going home, but I knew I wouldn't ever forget Greenbridge—the fountain in the square, the lonely cemetery at the end of Black Hill Road.

We decided to go into a shop called The Gingerbread Man and get something to eat while we waited for the bus. The rows of gingerbread men in the shop window had made me realize how hungry I was.

The Gingerbread Man was similar to the first shop—"Julie's shop" I called it in my mind. Besides the gingerbread men and jars of jams and jellies for sale, there were little gift items: painted china plates, boxes of incense, brass pots for plants. And over an

alcove at one side of the shop was a plaque that said
ANTIQUES.

The shop was not crowded, and as we stood
waiting for the salesgirl to wrap up our gingerbread
men, someone in the antiques area wound up a music
box. We could hear the rasping sound of the winding.

And then the delicate notes of the music box,
began a melody which we all knew.

> *Three blind mice*
> *Three blind mice*
> *See how they run*
> *See how they run*
> *They all ran after the farmer's wife*
> *She cut off their tails with the carving knife*
> *Did you ever see . . .*
> *As three blind mice.*

Those few notes were missing near the end. Just
as Julie always heard it in her mind.

She turned to me, her face white. As we listened
to the antique music box playing its tune, I could feel
my heart beating more rapidly.

When the tune was finished, it began again,
growing slower and slower as it wound down, until it
stopped in midtune with a last faint lingering note.

Chapter Five

The way things had worked out on our visit to Greenbridge that Saturday seemed truly amazing to me. It was really eerie to think of all that Julie and I had discovered in that one short afternoon.

First, before we had even figured out how to get to see the rooms behind the shop, we were practically whisked back there.

Next, we had solved the mystery of what had made Julie feel so fearful at the mention of Black Hill Road the day she was in Greenbridge with her mother.

Last but not least, we had found the music box that Julie must have heard when she was a little girl. No doubt it had been brightly painted then, but still with a defective mechanism that missed notes. When we found it in The Gingerbread Man, the paint was faded and the box looked a hundred years old—which I suppose it was, or close to. Whatever picture had been painted on the lid was too dim to make out.

"Do you want to buy it?" I had asked Julie, as we stood in the shop examining the worn little music box. It was silent now. The customer who had wound it up had moved on to look at other items. Julie's fingers trembled as she reached for the small brass key at the side of the box, but she didn't turn it. She just touched it, recapturing the feel of the key from years and years before.

"No," she said slowly, "I don't want to buy it." She set the box carefully back on a shelf and smiled at me. "I don't really want the memories, Allison. I just want to go home."

So we went home. But I couldn't get Green-bridge out of my mind.

Had Julie herself once owned that music box? Or was it one of the things for sale in the shop her family had owned? Maybe it had been her favorite thing in the shop and she wound it up to listen to it over and over again. *You'll have that worn out before we sell it*, her father would scold, but not too harshly. After all, Julie had been only a little girl. A little girl in high-buttoned shoes and other old-fashioned clothes. Pinafores. Sunbonnets. Itchy underwear and home-made mittens for cold winter days.

She went to a small schoolhouse, walking through falling snow on dark winter mornings. A very little girl. Six or seven. Bringing her lunch. And

Toddy would be at the school door, a big, hulking, bully of a boy. Eleven, maybe twelve.

What would he say to Julie as she came toward school? I didn't know what he would say, but I could imagine Julie—or whatever her name was then—trudging to school through the falling snow.

I made up a whole life for Julie in my mind.

In the cozy rooms behind the shop, Julie ate and dressed and studied her lessons. At bedtime she would go to her little upstairs bedroom with the windows overlooking the square. We might never know whether she owned the music box herself—but at least now we knew why "Three Blind Mice," sung around the campfire when Julie Whitcomb was eight years old, stirred her with feelings she couldn't understand.

School started. Our sophomore year. Everything was ragged around the edges, the way the first days of school are, and it was too hot for the back-to-school clothes everybody was wearing. My program got all goofed up with the computer scheduling, so I had three lunch periods and no English class. Miss Nicholson in the school office got sick and tired of seeing me before it all got straightened out. Greg Braden, whom I liked a lot, was in my science class, and that was about the best news of the whole first week.

But even with all the hassle, I still thought about Julie and her other life. Waiting in Miss Nicholson's office was a good time to think about things, and I did. How had Julie and I been so lucky as to find out so much so easily? That was a biggie, and I thought about it a lot in the days that followed our trip to Greenbridge.

I decided that if you were tracing your former life, doors miraculously opened for you, information fell at your feet, so to speak, as though it had only been waiting for your arrival.

And I learned other things. About a week after school started, a friend of Dad's came for dinner. He was an attorney. His name was William Armington, and he believed in reincarnation.

He came on a September evening that stayed light until amost seven and had the pleasant coolness of early autumn. The leaves were beginning to change and our yard was bordered by marigolds, red and gold and orange.

I helped Mom with dinner—a beef roast with mushrooms. When Mr. Armington, eating his roast beef, brought up the subject of reincarnation, I could hardly believe my ears. I stared across the table at him and thought about Julie and myself in Greenbridge. Reincarnation suddenly was everywhere I turned.

"Yes, indeed," Mr. Armington said, looking around the dinner table. "Reincarnation is real. I have known that for many years."

He was much older than Dad. His hair was thinning and his face had the usual signs of age. Once, I thought, he had been a very good-looking man. I knew Dad liked him, and as I looked across the table I liked him too. It wasn't hard. He had a kind face and intelligent eyes; he looked as though he knew *everything*.

"Reincarnation is the only answer," Mr. Armington said, gesturing with his fork. "Anyone can see there's more to do here on this earth than time to do it. There has to be more than one life for each of us."

Mom and Dad and Jimmy and I were all looking at Mr. Armington, and then Mom's voice drifted gently through the room: "I've always wanted to live in the days of the old castles. I suppose that's silly." She looked around at the rest of us self-consciously.

"Not at all," Mr. Armington said. "Feelings of attraction to certain places, certain times, are good indications that those places and times were parts of your experiences in former lives. And we've all had those, you know. Former lives."

He said it solemnly, as though it were the most natural comment anyone could make.

"I've always wanted to be a cowboy," Jimmy said, shoving a forkful of mashed potatoes into his mouth. He grinned at Mr. Armington as if they were old, old friends.

"Really?" Mom looked at Jimmy with surprise. "I thought you wanted to be an astronaut."

"That, too." Jimmy had a lot of interests.

Mr Armington smiled calmly. "I myself have always felt drawn to the time of the Russian Revolution," he said. "But I'm sure I've lived in other times as well."

He buttered a dinner roll and I watched him, feeling my fascination grow.

"Too bad we can't remember these former lives in detail," my father said. "I'd like to hear what life was really like in those old castles, for instance."

Mr. Armington reached for his water glass. Everything he did seemed very elegant to me.

"George is right," Mom said. "It's too bad we don't really know our former lives."

She turned toward Mr. Armington, and he smiled at her graciously. "Sometimes we can know," he said.

Between us, two pale yellow candles flickered their warm flamelight on the dinner table. I thought of the candles in the shop on Black Hill Road, all the golden flames in the colored glass cups. And I thought of the graveyard lying farther on down Black Hill Road, behind the tall iron fence. . . .

"The past *can* be recalled," Mr. Armington said, nodding at Mom. "There are people who have been able, under the proper conditions, to remember many former lives."

"Many lives?" Mom didn't like that. I could understand what she was feeling. The identity she thought of as "I" was threatened, splintered and cast back into the past, into times and places she couldn't even remember. She might like castles, but she really wanted to be one person, have one life, *this* life.

"I don't want to live a lot of other lives." Mom looked over at me for support. "What do you think about all this, Allison?"

Dad looked at me too, and I could see Mr.

Armington watching me with a twinkle in his eye. He was loving the conversation, I thought.

"Do you *really* believe in reincarnation?" I looked at him steadily.

"I do sincerely believe in reincarnation," Mr. Armington said. "It explains so many things, you see." He looked at me with the manner of a teacher at school patiently explaining math problems to a student. "Our dreams, for one thing." He lifted his eyes and looked around the table at Mom and Dad and Jimmy. "Some of our dreams—not all—but some of our dreams come from lingering memories of other lives."

I thought of the bird fluttering in the cage hung in a wide window through which sunlight streamed. I put my finger through the bars and the little bird came and perched there. It was a fleeting thought, gone in a moment, but I was filled with happiness. Could I ever tell anyone how I so often dreamed about the little bird in the cage by the window, or expect anyone to understand the happiness I always felt at this simple thing?

I wondered if Julie ever dreamed about Greenbridge. . . .

"Reincarnation also explains our feelings of affinity with certain people, why we like some more than others. It explains our attraction to or our sense of feeling comfortable in certain places."

There was a pause while everybody took this in.

"And it certainly explains prodigies," Mr. Armington continued. "The genius of Mozart, for example."

He looked around to see if everyone was in agreement with this.

Mom had finished eating. She was sitting with her elbows on the table, her fingers laced together and her chin resting on them.

Dad was still eating. "Mozart?" He poised his fork and glanced across the table at Mr. Armington.

"Mozart wrote a piano concerto at five," Mr. Armington said, with enthusiasm. "At the age of six he was playing for the crowned heads of Europe. How could this be? Perhaps it was because he had lived other lives and had already perfected his musical talent."

The dining room was silent. I could see that my father was listening closely. He put down his fork and pushed his plate away.

"Yes, indeed, reincarnation explains so many things." Mr. Armington urged us to believe with him, to explore new ideas. "The more you think about it, the more ludicrous the inadequacy of one life span begins to seem."

No one said anything.

Mr. Armington took a new approach. "Consider the King Tut exhibit," he said thoughtfully.

"The King Tut exhibit?" Mom looked at Mr. Armington curiously.

Mr. Armington smiled at her. "Crowds of people waited for hours and hours and *hours* to see the treasures from King Tutankamen's tomb. They waited in bad weather, and in the dark night hours, before the museum doors were even open. Why did they do this? In every city the exhibit was shown, the attendance was phenomenal."

"What's that got to do with reincarnation?" Jimmy wanted to know. He stopped eating and watched Mr. Armington.

"I believe," Mr. Armington said gravely, "that if we have lived former lives at various times in history, the further back we go the more these lives converge. I believe that many of us lived during the times of ancient Egypt. Therefore, an exhibit of Egyptian treasures stirs subconscious memories. When artifacts of our former lives appear as historical exhibits, we respond with an interest that, on the surface, seems unusual."

I fussed with a sprig of parsley on my plate, thinking of Julie's other life. It was a lot closer in time than ancient Egypt.

"Do you mean maybe I was once an Egyptian prince?" Jimmy asked with a grin.

"You may well have been," Mr. Armington assured him.

"But what about all the years between?" Mom said. (A good question, I thought.) "What happens during all those years?"

Mr. Armington regarded Mom serenely. "There aren't always so many years between reincarnations. Some people return very quickly, within the same century."

"The same century?" My father was surprised. But Mr. Armington replied, "Easily, easily."

There were a thousand questions I wanted to ask,

but my tongue felt glued to the roof of my mouth. Black Hill Road, the flickering candles of Candlewick, the notes of the music box song, all swam around me in the calm of the dining room.

"Everything is delicious." Mr. Armington smiled at Mom.

What if we started talking about something else? I thought helplessly. There was so much more I wanted to learn from Mr. Armington, but I didn't want to appear too eager. *Oh, don't stop now,* I begged silently.

Mr. Armington patted his mouth with the corner of his napkin.

"People who have been murdered, for instance," he said. "It is my belief that murdered people return rather quickly, as though perhaps life owes them something." He glanced around the table.

As though life owes them something. His words echoed in my mind. That was something to think about.

"Well, we don't know anything about murdered people," Mom said.

"I'll be honest," my father said apologetically. "I'm afraid I'm just not convinced that people can be reincarnated." He seemed puzzled that Mr. Armington could take it all so seriously.

"I'm not sure I like the idea," Mom admitted.

Jimmy wriggled in his chair. "Aw, come on, you guys. Maybe I really was a cowboy once."

Mr. Armington looked at me across the table, between the candles, and we smiled.

That night I made a list of all that we had talked about at dinner. Mozart. King Tut's exhibit. Dreams. Murdered people. All of it. I knew Julie would want to know, and I made the list so I wouldn't forget anything.

Nothing Mr. Armington had said supported my idea that when you are tracing a former life doors open for you. But I added that to my list anyway. It was something I felt I had discovered for myself, witnessed first hand. Maybe Mr. Armington didn't even know about it. Of all the facts on my list, I considered it one of the most important to keep in mind.

I thought about showing the list to Julie the next day at school. We were in homeroom together, but I knew there wouldn't be enough time to discuss my list, or any chance in the third-period English class we had together. Lunch would give us the time, but there would be other people at the table, and anyway the cafeteria was too noisy a place to talk about something this serious.

As I composed the list and read it over, I grew more and more eager to show it to Julie. If she could just come to school a few minutes early . . . Although it was late, I dialed her number, listening to the ring at the other end of the line. *Come on, come on,* I thought impatiently. *Isn't anybody home!*

Then Julie answered.

"Can you come to school about fifteen minutes early tomorrow?" I asked, getting right to the point.

"Sure, I guess so." Julie sounded puzzled. "What's up?"

"I've got something real interesting to show you," I said. "A lot of things I found out about reincarnation. Meet me at the bench at eight-fifteen, okay?"

The bench was a long concrete bench at one side of the high school lawn, a popular meeting place before and after classes.

Julie hesitated, then said, "Let's make it by the gym entrance."

I didn't care where we met.

"The gym entrance," I agreed. "Eight-fifteen."

Chapter Six

The next morning I dressed for school quickly. Blue cotton sweater, jeans, copper earrings. The earrings were new, and I had to admire myself a moment in the mirror. There was a certain flush of expectation on my face, an extra brightness in the blue-green eyes reflected back at me in the mirror. And it wasn't just that blue tops look good on blue-eyed blondes. It was something more. It was my own sense of excitement, a sense of adventure waiting just around the corner. Julie didn't know it yet, but I was going to talk her into going back to Greenbridge again.

I gathered up my books and my list, and I was at the gym entrance by five after eight. A couple of guys going in early said, "Hi, cutie," and I wished one of them had been Greg Braden.

GREG BRADEN: *A boy who doesn't know
Allison Morley is alive.*

More and more kids came past me into school as
the time went by, but Julie wasn't among them.

Eight-fifteen. Eight-twenty.

"Hi, Allison." A girl named Joanne McKinney
ran up to me, swinging her book bag. She settled in
beside me at the gym door, like she was going to stay
forever.

"Hi, Joanne." I wished she'd just go on into
school.

"I like your earrings," Joanne said.

"Thanks." Already my time to talk to Julie was
running out. I didn't need Joanne McKinney hanging
around.

"Come on, Joanne, we'll be late." Cindy Norris,
Joanne's best friend, came along. She brushed past
me, beckoning to Joanne. "Hi, Allison!" she called
over her shoulder.

"Hi. . . ." Joanne and Cindy were gone. Thank
goodness. I was alone again with my list, waiting for
Julie.

Eight-twenty-five. Eight-twenty-seven. I waited
for Julie until the absolute last minute. Then I ran
through the corridors and up two flights of stairs, and
barely reached my homeroom before the bell rang.

Mrs. Bremmer was already at the front desk with
her attendance book. I sat down and turned a little in
my seat so I could watch the door. I planned to give
Julie a "Where *were* you?" look when she came in.

Announcements droned around me like weary bees, and some idiot sent a paper airplane flying when Mrs. Bremmer's back was turned. Very third grade. I scowled across the room. Life is serious, Eddie Farley, get with it.

At first I thought Julie was going to come in late, but by lunch period I knew she wasn't in school at all. I called her from the pay phone in the hall by the cafeteria.

"Julie?"

"Oh—hi, Allison."

She didn't sound too bad. "What's wrong?" I asked. "Why aren't you at school?"

"I—I woke up with a sore throat this morning," she said falteringly.

"A sore throat now? I thought people got sore throats in the winter."

I felt impatient. I had three more classes, and all I wanted to do was see Julie and show her my list.

"I'll come by after school," I said. "I've got something to show you, remember? About you-know-what."

"Yeah," Julie said with a sigh.

I hung up the phone and stood for a moment watching the kids stream through the hall, talking, carrying books, opening lockers. And I thought about Greenbridge and Julie's life there, so different from anything these kids were living now.

There are other days, other times you don't know anything about, I told them silently.

There are rooms and clothes and people you don't know anything about.

There are places you don't know anything about.

Places like Greenbridge eighty years ago.

Places like graveyards after dark.

I stood thinking those thoughts, watching the students go to their classes. I knew the bell was going to ring soon, and finally I gathered up my books from the ledge by the phone and walked slowly to my history class.

Mr. Garcia was my history teacher. He was one of the nicest teachers I had ever had, a small, dapper man with sympathetic brown eyes. Lots of girls in the history class had crushes on him. I did, too, a little. But this day I had other things on my mind.

Gwen Phillips was giving a long, involved answer to a question about the Industrial Revolution. She always had the right answers. Mr. Garcia called on her a lot. As I listened to Gwen, my gaze drifted to the window and across the school grounds. A circular flowerbed was planted near the long bench where I had wanted to meet Julie. A few yards away, a bronze plaque on a cement pedestal had been erected in memory of a man named John Westman who had donated the money for the new wing of the high school, back when Julie and I were still in grade school.

I looked at the bright autumn flowers and the bronze plaque.

Gwen finished speaking and sat down.

"Thank you," Mr. Garcia said in his soft, calm voice. "Now we will turn to page one hundred nine."

I opened my book, but I kept looking outside. The plaque with its inscription reminded me of the gravestones in Greenbridge Cemetery. Julie had said she had gone to the cemetery once at night. I tried to imagine what that would be like . . . wind stirring the grass beside the gravestones, whispering through the bare branches of trees; darkness stretching into darkness; and when clouds parted, moonlight shining pale upon the grave markers . . . Albert Evans, beloved husband of Sarah . . . Martha Colridge, the Lord is my shepherd—I will dwell in the house of the Lord forever . . . names, dates, epitaphs, ghostly in the darkness as the wind moved in the grass along the invisible paths.

It would be scary, all right. And Julie had been a very little girl. What if a hand reached up, clutching at you from a grave? What if a coffin resting by a freshly dug grave creaked open and someone . . . something . . . stepped out into the darkness beside you?

Julie had said a bunch of kids had gone to the graveyard one night, and I pictured a small, straggling group of children, freckle-faced boys, girls with pigtails; five, six, maybe seven of them, following Toddy to the cemetery on Black Hill Road, trying to act brave while their knees knocked together and their palms grew sweaty with fear. . . . *You're scared to go!* Toddy taunted them. *We're not! We're not! . . . Well, if you're not scared, follow me.*

Toddy would go first, looking back over his shoulder to be sure the little kids were still coming along behind him. They had sneaked out of their houses. . . . *If Mama knew we were going to the cemetery she wouldn't like it.* But Toddy didn't care about that. He probably wouldn't even get scolded for daring the little kids to go into the cemetery at night. Julie said nobody scolded Toddy.

A cloud moved across the school lawn, and the sun that had been shining on the plaque and the flowerbed was gone. There was no one at the meeting bench, and in the bleakness of the sunless light the bench looked forlorn and faraway.

When I got to Julie's house after school, she was in the living room watching a soap opera.

"How's your throat?"

"A lot better." Julie switched off the TV and finger-combed her hair with an absent gesture. Across the room was the piano where she had picked out "Three Blind Mice" that warm August afternoon. Someone had put the cover over the piano keys. On the table by the chair where Julie had been sitting I could see an empty ice cream dish. Being sick was hard work!

"Allison, how are you, dear?" Julie's mother came into the living room. "You're looking wonderful. It's nice of you to come and see Julie today. She should be back to school tomorrow."

Mrs. Whitcomb loved to talk, but I only wanted to talk to Julie.

"How is the new semester going for you?" Mrs. Whitcomb settled lightly, like a butterfly, on the arm of Julie's chair.

"Pretty well," I said. I forced my attention back to Riverton High. "I've got some good teachers this year."

In the kitchen, the telephone rang.

"Excuse me, you two." Mrs. Whitcomb went to answer the phone.

"Let's go up to your room," I said to Julie as soon as her mother was gone. "I have to talk to you—alone."

Julie didn't look very enthused, but she followed me.

"You stayed home on purpose," I accused her as we went up the stairs. "I have this terrific list I want to show you. Aren't you even curious about what I found out?"

I didn't wait for an answer. I hurried into Julie's room, tossed my books and sweater on the bed and got the list out of the pocket of my jeans. "Come on," I urged, sitting on the edge of the bed. "Come on and look at this."

I unfolded the list, smoothed it out and laid it on the bedspread.

"Maybe that's you," I said, pointing my finger to number six on the list.

Murdered people come back soon.

Julie looked at me uncertainly. "Do you think I was murdered?"

"Maybe," I replied. "You said something awful

happened to you. What's more awful than murder? And you said you thought you never grew up in Greenbridge."

Julie looked at the list.

"I added this myself," I said, pointing to the last item.

Doors open when you are tracing a former life.

"How do you know that?" Julie looked up from the list.

"Isn't it obvious?" I asked. "We only went to Greenbridge one time, *one time*, and look at all the things we found out. We know practically all about you: that your family owned a store and you lived there in the rooms behind the store. You probably helped out in the store as much as a little girl could, or you played there sometimes. Now and then you went to visit some friend or relative who lived on one of the farms nearby, and you played in the barn. In the winter you went sledding there.

"There was some horrid boy, a neighborhood bully, who played jokes on everybody and teased little kids into doing scary things like going into the cemetery at night.

"I can see your whole life."

Julie listened to everything I said with a tense expression.

"I can see your whole life," I said again.

"You do understand, don't you." Julie looked up at me gratefully. "You understand just how it was."

After all the years of keeping memories and strange fears to herself, I could see it was a tremendous relief to Julie to have someone understand the way she felt.

"I think it's very exciting," I said. "But I think we ought to go back to Greenbridge—"

Julie started to shake her head before I even finished what I was saying.

"I don't want to go back, Allison. I knew you'd want to do that. I don't feel right when I'm in Greenbridge. I feel scared all over again. I don't like remembering how scared I was. I didn't want to see your list, I didn't want to learn more about reincarnation. I just wanted someone to understand."

"Now, wait, let me finish." I hurried on before she could make any more objections. "Think of all we learned in just that one visit. Aren't you even curious to see what else we could find out? Maybe we could find out what really happened to you. Wouldn't you like to know what happened to you? It's not going to hurt you, after all."

Julie hesitated, looking at me helplessly. She didn't really know *what* she wanted. At least she didn't know at that moment, there in her room in Riverton on a sunny September afternoon. Her life in Greenbridge didn't seem real then. It had faded into some hazy place she didn't like.

"Sometimes I want to know," she said cautiously. "And other times I don't even want to think about it, and I really wish I wouldn't remember things."

"Once more, anyway," I urged. "Let's go back at least one more time. Maybe that woman who owns that shop now can tell us something about the people who used to own it. I know there might have been lots of owners over the years, but maybe we could trace back somehow and—"

Julie was shaking her head again. "I don't think that woman wants to see us again, and I don't think she'd be happy about answering a lot of questions."

I had to agree with Julie about that. The woman at Martha-Ann Gifts wouldn't want to answer our questions. "Okay," I said. "Could we just go back and walk around? Maybe we could go inside the cemetery. Maybe some of the names on the gravestones would mean something to you."

Julie looked startled. "What if I saw my own name?" she whispered.

I had thought of that. But I didn't want to sound too morbid, so I said, "You don't know what your name was. How could you find it?"

We looked at each other silently, and Julie finally folded up my list and handed it back to me.

"Saturday?" I asked.

"All right," Julie agreed with defeat. "It seems like I'm always getting taken to that cemetery when I don't really want to go."

"Julie!" I scolded her. "Toddy dared you to go there because he was mean. I'm trying to help."

"I know," Julie said with a faint smile. "I just hope we're doing the right thing."

Chapter Seven

.

On Saturday Julie and I caught the bus for Greenbridge. But we almost didn't go. There had been rain during the night, and the Saturday morning sky was overcast and threatening.

"It looks like a good day to stay home," Mom said at breakfast. The view from the kitchen windows was bleak, and any other time I would have agreed with her: it was a good day to stay home, read, pop popcorn, watch TV, listen to records. But this wasn't any other time.

The phone rang while I was still eating breakfast, and I didn't faint with surprise when Mom said, "It's for you, Allison—Julie."

I took the kitchen extension.

"Allison? It's going to rain. My mom thinks I'm crazy to want to go way off to Greenbridge today."

I had to think about that for a minute. I knew
Julie had mixed feelings about going back to Greenbridge and she wouldn't mind too much if the rain
called off our trip. I could handle Julie's mixed
feelings, but I didn't want other people—her mom,
for one—getting suspicious about our trips there. And
what if my mom suddenly said, "Good gracious,
Allison, you're not going to Greenbridge on a day like
this, are you?"

I looked at Mom and Dad and Jimmy and tried to
figure out something to say to Julie that wouldn't
sound suspicious.

PRIVACY: *Something that's hard to get when
your whole family is three feet away.*

I leaned close to the phone and whispered, "Tell
your mom I want to get something special I saw
there—present for my dad. His birthday is coming
up." (My dad's birthday was in March; I was shopping
early.)

I could hear Julie making these explanations at
her end of the line, and I glanced nonchalantly over
my shoulder. No one at the breakfast table was paying
the least bit of attention to me or my phone
conversation. Mom and Dad were teasing Jimmy
about how much maple syrup he poured on his
pancakes (a whole river of syrup).

"Allison?" Julie came back on the line. "Okay,"
she said, "we'll go. I'll meet you at the bus stop."

* * *

The early days of September had begun to color the leaves on the elm trees that bordered the town square in Greenbridge, and the cobbled streets were plastered with damp yellow leaves.

Julie and I bought taffy apples at The Gingerbread Man and sat on a bench in the square to eat them before starting for the cemetery. The last person we wanted to see was the lady from Martha-Ann Gifts. But as we sat in the square, we saw her hurrying along with an umbrella under her arm.

She was across the square, in no way close enough to speak to us, but she saw us and frowned to herself and kept eyeing us as she went toward her shop. Then she disappeared inside.

"She makes me feel like a criminal or something," Julie said crossly, wadding up the paper napkin that had been wrapped around the taffy-apple stick.

"We're not doing anything wrong," I said defiantly. But I was glad we had decided not to go back into Martha-Ann Gifts to ask any more questions.

"Let's get started," I said. "Do you feel drawn to any particular street?"

Julie looked around vaguely and shook her head.

"Then let's start out to Black Hill Road and see if you get some more memories at the cemetery."

"Okay." Julie stood up and stuffed her hands in the pockets of her denim jacket. "Let's go."

I got up, too, and we crossed the square, went past the public library and the beautiful old homes, crossed the bridge where the waters murmured gently. We passed the area of the new shops, and then the cemetery was just ahead. We walked toward it in the gloomy light.

The cemetery gate was open, but no cars were parked nearby, and we couldn't see anyone in the cemetery. The paths were empty, spattered with wet leaves. Julie and I looked at each other like conspirators as we went through the open gate into the leaf-strewn paths of the graveyard.

Almost at once we were startled by a voice. A middle-aged man wearing overalls and a workman's cap appeared from a cluster of tall bushes near the gate.

"Going to rain again," he said cheerfully. "I don't see many visitors on rainy days."

Julie and I exchanged glances. We hadn't expected to meet the caretaker.

"We just wanted to walk around," I said. Suddenly I wondered if we were allowed to come in. Maybe you were supposed to have some real family grave to visit if you came into the cemetery.

The caretaker squinted up at the dark sky. "Go right ahead," he said, "if you don't mind gettin' wet. The gate's open till five o'clock. Then I lock up."

I looked over at the tall black iron gate. At five o'clock it would be locked. Nobody outside could come in.

But Toddy had brought the little kids in after dark.

Was the gate open then?

If the gate was locked, how did they get in?

"Do you always close at five o'clock?" I asked.

The caretaker was raking at a strip of grass beside the gate. Fragile wet leaves caught in the prongs of the rake.

"Five o'clock as long as I can remember."

I backed away, watching as he scratched at the grass. It was still early afternoon.

"We'll be gone long before five o'clock," I told him.

"Okay." The caretaker stopped raking for a moment and straightened up. "You want to see something pretty, you go on over to the new section." He motioned to the left. "We've got some real nice flowers over there."

Julie stood close to me. I could feel her tension. She was looking around the cemetery as if she expected to see ghosts rising from the graves.

"Oh . . . the new section," I said, nodding vaguely.

"This over here's the old section." The caretaker motioned to the right and toward the back of the grounds. "You can see the difference," he said with assurance.

"Oh, of course," I said, as if I knew all about cemeteries.

But there was a difference. We could see it, Julie and I, as we wandered along. The old section was weedy, overgrown around the graves. There were no flowers at the headstones, only the graves with their stone markers—like the bronze memorial plaque at school.

"Julie—" I stopped walking and looked at the gravestones.

"What?"

"I was just thinking how you never like to meet me by the bench at school. I think it's because the bench is right by that Westman memorial thing and it reminds you of a gravestone. It reminds you of this place."

Julie leaned against a tree trunk and surveyed the area around her. "I think you're right," she said at last. "The plaque at school *is* a lot like these gravestones. And I never liked that plaque. I didn't know why I didn't like it, I just never did. Every time I went by it I felt"—she hesitated—"I felt unhappy, like something had suddenly gone wrong with the day."

We were both quiet for a few moments. The caretaker was out of sight somewhere, lost behind shrubs or trees.

Finally I said, "How did you get in that night, the night you came with Toddy and the other little kids?"

Julie didn't answer.

"You must have come after the gate closed. You said you came when it was dark. Was there a gate then?"

Julie stared into the distance. She looked across the grass, across the tombstones, across the gloomy light that lay upon the paths. "Yes," she said, "there was a gate. It was closed."

"Then how did you get in?"

It seemed a long time before she answered me. She was trying to remember.

"There was a broken place. Toddy had found it; he knew it was there. We went in, following Toddy, and then we . . ." Julie paused, thinking back to a place and a time I had never known.

I wanted to shout, "What happened?" but I was afraid to break the thin thread of memory holding Julie to that past time, that dark night so many years ago which she was remembering now.

Julie started speaking again, slowly, like someone feeling her way on unfamiliar ground.

"We began to move around through the cemetery, to show Toddy we weren't afraid. We all stayed together, holding hands. It was so dark, I couldn't see Toddy anymore. And then there was a sort of low, moaning sound somewhere in the dark, somewhere very close."

I could feel my skin prickle. A twig fell from a branch above me, brushing my cheek. I let out a little shriek, and Julie and I plastered ourselves against the iron fence. We giggled nervously. Then Julie continued her story.

"One of the kids screamed, 'It's a ghost!' and we all began screaming and running every which way."

It's a ghost! . . . It's a ghost! . . . Shrieks of frightened little children rang in my ears. I heard their cries, wavering, terror-filled . . . *It's a ghost! . . . It's a ghost!*

Julie was silent. We moved away from the fence and wandered among the graves.

She can't stop now, I thought. What happened after the children panicked and scattered in the dark?

"What did you do?" I wanted to ask, but I didn't. Julie had such an odd, distant look in her eyes, I was afraid if I spoke I would break the spell she was under.

Yellow leaves fluttered down from the trees.

I could see cars going by on Black Hill Road beyond the bars of the iron fence.

"I wasn't holding anybody's hand anymore," Julie said slowly, "I was just running to get away from the ghost."

What happened! I thought frantically.

Julie was silent so long, I broke the rule I had made not to distract her.

"What happened then?" I blurted out.

The words seemed to echo in the silence of the graveyard. *What happened then? What happened then?*

"Then . . . ?" Julie's voice faltered, and she looked at me with a confused expression. The thread of memory was broken. "I guess I just ran home."

"Oh." It was a letdown. "Well," I said after a moment, "are you getting any more memories about anything, now that we're here?"

"No, I'm not." She looked around with a slight shiver. "I hate these damp days," she said. "Let's go."

I felt depressed, too, in the silent, deserted graveyard, and I followed Julie as she started back toward the entrance.

We said good-bye to the caretaker and went out through the tall black gate. It was still a long way until five o'clock, when the gate would be locked. A small boy with a dark summer tan ran along the outside of the cemetery, holding a stick against the iron palings of the fence. *Rat-tat-tat-tat-tat.* The dull clink of the stick against the fence was almost lost in the oppressive air of the afternoon. I had walked for several steps before I realized that Julie was not beside me.

I turned and looked back to where she stood in the shadow of the gate. She was watching the boy running as he held the stick against the bars of the cemetery fence; I had never seen her look so anxious.

"Julie?" I walked back to where she stood. "What's wrong?"

"I don't know," she said faintly. "I just thought I ought to stop him. He shouldn't be doing that."

I looked over my shoulder. The boy was almost out of sight, and I turned back to Julie. "Why did you think you should stop him?"

"Oh, Allison, I don't know. For a moment he made me remember something, or almost remember. But it's gone now, whatever it was."

"Try to remember," I urged, but she shook her head.

"It's gone, Allison. It's just gone."

We walked back along Black Hill Road, and we were lucky: the rain held off. The wind was rising, and tree branches tossed against the sky. Our hair blew across our faces. But the rain held off.

At the bus stop we went into the little station to wait. There was only one bench inside and some women were already sitting on it, so Julie and I stood by the door and watched for the bus. At last we saw it coming, bright beams from the headlights glowing in the dim afternoon.

I went up the steps onto the bus after Julie and followed her down the aisle to seats halfway back.

Maybe we would never return to Greenbridge.

Julie rested her head against the bus seat and closed her eyes.

Farmhouses sped past. Wooden rail fences and cows in pastures.

But Julie didn't want to see them. She was exhausted from remembering, from being in Greenbridge.

I sat beside her, awake, alert. I looked at every farmhouse that passed and wondered if it was the one where Julie climbed to the loft to play.

Soon the farms faded into the distance. Soon we would be home.

I nudged Julie. "How do you feel?"

She smiled. "Okay, I guess."

Then we were silent again, and I thought about what she had said back at the cemetery.

I guess I just ran home.

At first, that seemed a logical conclusion to the adventure: separated from the others, scared out of her wits in the spooky old cemetery, Julie had just run home.

Very logical.

And yet there was something I didn't totally accept about that. Could a frightened little girl think calmly and clearly enough in the midst of panic to find her way back through a pitch-dark, unfamiliar place to just the right spot where the loose bar was in the row of iron palings?

I looked out at the scenery which was growing familiar as we neared Riverton. There was the shopping center . . . Burger King . . . Stereo City.

The bus zoomed along, and the first raindrops began to hit the windowpanes.

I thought of the deserted cemetery lanes back in Greenbridge, rain spattering down through the trees, darkening the headstones, slowly at first, then with growing force until the gravestones streamed with rain, glistening in the fading light.

I guess I just ran home.

But I wondered.

I wondered if it had really been that way.

Chapter Eight

"Allison and her friend Julie went to Greenbridge a few days ago—puts me in the mood to go myself."

I could hear Mom talking to one of her friends on the phone. It was my turn to do the dinner dishes, and Mom had just brought the empty dessert plates from the dining room when the phone rang, so she'd answered it in the kitchen. Through the windows over the sink I could see the evening already growing dark.

Yes, Julie and I had been in Greenbridge, all right. How surprised Mom would have been if she'd known the real reason we went there.

"Monday?" I heard Mom say. "Yes, that's good for me. Let's go then."

When she hung up the phone she said, "You've

inspired me, honey. Vera Lawrence and I are going to Greenbridge next Monday. Neither of us has been in ages."

"That's great," I said, swishing the dishes through the dishwater. "Have fun."

Just as I was finishing the dishes, Jimmy came into the kitchen to get a bowl of pretzels. Dinner had been over for nearly half an hour, so naturally he was starved again. I was thinking about Greenbridge as we went to the living room and I sat down on the arm of the couch to check the TV schedule. Nothing looked very interesting—certainly not the 1947 detective movie Jimmy was watching. Around me were the familiar sights and sounds of after-dinner, of evenings at home I had lived through hundreds of times before. Only this time I was thinking about Greenbridge Cemetery and Black Hill Road. And I didn't usually sit around the house after dinner thinking about graveyards.

BLACK HILL ROAD: A *street leading to a place you don't want to go.*

"Hey, Allison?" Jimmy turned toward me, cramming a pretzel into his mouth. "Do you think this guy really did it?"

"I don't know," I said, hoping that my thoughtful voice sounded as if I had been watching, paying attention. "Do *you* think he did it?" The ball's in your court, I thought, as Jimmy twisted back toward the TV screen with a shrug of his shoulders.

A newsbreak and a quickie weather report came on. I stared without interest at the overview of the United States and a swirl of lines showing where rain was falling.

Outside it was dark. On Black Hill Road the cemetery gate would be closed and locked for the night, the dead people all sleeping under the grass as the night wore on. I knew I should go upstairs and study, but I didn't want to be alone just then. It was comforting to see Mom glancing through the evening paper, Dad lazily watching the detective program, Jimmy sitting cross-legged on the floor with his bowl of pretzels. I thought I'd stay awhile with them and not go upstairs and be alone.

On Monday morning Mom was still sitting at the kitchen table when I was ready to leave for school. At ten o'clock Mrs. Lawrence would stop by to pick her up, and they would drive to Greenbridge.

Dad was just leaving, too, so Jimmy and I got a ride. We dropped Jimmy at Lincoln Elementary, which looked smaller and smaller to me every time I went by. When I was in school there it had seemed so big, the playground spreading around the school as far as the eye could see. Now it was nothing. A gravelly plot of ground and an asphalt area near the school doors, where we had drawn hopscotch squares and jumped rope.

"'Bye!" Jimmy slammed the car door and sprinted away, spotting his buddies somewhere in a throng of kids who all looked alike to me.

Dad and I drove on in silence. When we pulled up in front of Riverton High, I was ready to jump out; Dad never had extra time in the mornings.

" 'Bye." Like Jimmy, I hurried away from the car into my world of school.

"See you tonight," Dad called after me, and I turned and waved as the car pulled away from the curb.

I had already told Julie that my mom and Mrs. Lawrence were going to Greenbridge, and when I met her in the cafeteria at lunch period I reminded her that this was the day.

"She said we inspired her," I remarked wryly, biting into the sandwich I had brought from home.

Julie smiled. "I hope she has a good time," she said.

"She'll have a good time."

Julie had classes later in the afternoon than I did, so I walked home alone that day. I felt restless, as though something was going to happen. But I couldn't think what it might be. The day so far had been as routine as ever, even to the note Mom had left on the kitchen table:

> *To whom it may concern* (Mom's joke)
> *I'll be home by about four-thirty. Don't eat*
> *everything in the house before I get there.* (That
> was for Jimmy.)

I got a Coke and went upstairs to my room. When I heard Mom call, "Hello! I'm home," I ran downstairs to see what she'd bought. She was hanging her coat in the hall closet, and she turned and smiled at me as I came down the stairs.

Jimmy was on his way out the front door, a baseball cap pushed down over his eyes. "See you guys later," he said, not interested in the packages Mom had brought home from Greenbridge.

"You be home by five-thirty," Mom reminded him, and there was just time to hear his disgusted, "Aw, Mom, that early?" before the door closed behind him.

"What did you buy?"

I came down the last few steps and eyed the cluster of small parcels on the hall table. I wondered if Mom might possibly have gone to Candlewick, or if she had bought anything at Martha-Ann Gifts.

"Some really pretty things," Mom said. "Let's go into the kitchen. I can show you while I start dinner."

I helped her carry the packages, and we spread them out on the kitchen table. There was an address book with a leather cover, and a beautiful metal box painted with flowers and birds, just right for keeping jewelry in. There was fresh homemade bread and a bag of blueberry muffins from one of the bakeshops.

"We had the loveliest lunch," Mom said as we unwrapped the things she had bought—nothing from Candlewick or Martha-Ann Gifts. "Ah," she said, "here's my special thing."

From a small white cardboard box she lifted a delicate china candy dish wrapped in tissue paper.

"Isn't this lovely?" she said enthusiastically.

It was a beautiful little dish, and Mom held it carefully, turning it this way and that to admire the fluted sides and gold rim.

"That's really nice," I said.

The cardboard box had the same name of the shop printed on the lid:

T. RENDLEY

ANTIQUES HANDCRAFTS

FINE CHINA

I didn't remember seeing that particular shop, but there were so many shops in Greenbridge that Julie and I hadn't been to all of them.

"A very old couple run the shop," Mom said, still admiring her dish. "They must be a hundred. Well," she laughed at her own exaggeration, "in their eighties anyway."

She set the dish on the table and swept the muffins away. "These are for breakfast," she said, "but we'll have some of this wonderful homemade bread for dinner tonight."

I listened absently, opening and closing the cover of the white cardboard box. An old couple . . . in their eighties. T. Rendley . . . could that be T. for Tod . . . ?

No, that was really stretching things, I decided. I had Toddy on my mind. I began to help Mom with dinner, but my restless mood persisted, the edgy, expectant feeling that you have sometimes on hot summer days when it's going to rain but the first drops haven't fallen yet and the air vibrates with waiting for the storm.

Chapter Nine

I think I always knew Julie and I would find out what happened to her in that other life. I think I always knew that suddenly one day she would remember whatever bad thing had happened to her and why all her memories were only of childhood.

I thought we would go back to Greenbridge, maybe not tomorrow or next week, but sometime. It seemed inevitable that we would go back. Someday we would be standing on a certain street in Greenbridge and she would remember; or we would turn just the right corner; or walk into just the right shop and see some special thing; and the terrible, final memory would come back to her.

I was right, in a way. The final memory came. Only I had been wrong about where and how it came.

We weren't in Greenbridge at all. We weren't even together. It was that very night, the evening after Mom had been to Greenbridge. Julie was at home doing homework, and I was home, in my room, doing homework, too. Mom was not too tired from her trip to go with Dad and Jimmy to a Parents' Night at Lincoln Elementary.

"We won't be late," Mom said.

Jimmy was fidgeting around in the blue trousers he had to wear on special occasions like Parents' Nights.

Dad fished the car keys out of his pocket, and then they were gone.

I had the house to myself—and that turned out to be fortunate, although I have to admit that at first I was kind of scared when the doorbell began to ring so insistently . . . *ring ring ring rinnnng* with hardly a pause between. I looked up from my book and sat absolutely still for a moment. The sound of the bell filled the whole house. Something awful must have happened, I thought as I moved at last and ran down the stairs through the deserted house. Just as I reached the bottom of the stairs the sound of someone knocking frantically on the door joined the steady ring of the bell.

"Who is it?" I called. I was too nervous to open the door even with the safety chain on.

"It's me—it's me—" Julie's voice was so strained and agitated I hardly recognized it.

"Julie?" I fumbled with the locks and swung the door open.

My folks had left the porch light on, and Julie stood in the glare of the light, flushed and breathless. She had no jacket or sweater, and I knew she had run all the way from her house to mine. Her hair was windblown, and she was clutching a book to her chest as though it might get away from her and escape into the night. Her knuckles were white, and her fingers were clenched tight around the cover of the book.

"Julie! What is it!" I held the door wider and she darted into the hallway. She looked as if she was going to burst into tears, and her eyes had a wild brightness.

"I remember what happened! Oh, Allison, *I remember.*"

The words came rushing out, and for a moment I just stood and stared at her as the realization of what she was saying swept over me.

"You remember?" I felt a surge of excitement and a tingling sensation along the skin of my arms.

"Yes, *yes.* I remember what happened, how it all ended—" Her voice broke off with a gasping sob and tears sprang into her eyes. "Oh, Allison." She was crying now and shivering with cold.

"My gosh! Honest? You really remember?" I pulled her through the hallway toward the stairs. I wasn't sure how soon Mom and Dad and Jimmy would be back. Evening affairs at grade school were never late; they could be back any minute. I could imagine the fuss and the questions if they saw Julie like this.

"It's here—it's in this book—" Julie was trying to tell me as I dragged her along. I wanted to hear it all, every word, right from the beginning, but first I had to get her up to my room where we could have some privacy. "Come on, Julie. Hurry, come on upstairs. You can tell me upstairs," I begged as she stumbled along, blinded by her tears.

I was sure that when we were only halfway up the stairs, the front door would open and Jimmy would come running in and I'd hear Dad or Mom call, "We're home, Allison," before they all stopped short with amazement to see Julie Whitcomb with her windblown hair and tear-streaked face, holding a book in a deathgrip in her hands.

But the door remained closed in the hallway below, and Julie and I reached the top of the stairs. I practically pushed her into my room, and then I closed the door and stood braced against it as though even then we weren't quite safe and some invisible force would come through the door and stop us before Julie could tell me what it was she had remembered, what it was that had terrified her and sent her running through the dark streets to my house.

Julie was still trying to talk through her hysterical sobs and tears. "It's here—in the book."

The book she held toward me trembled violently in her grasp. It was her American literature book from school, a red cover with black print. I had one just like it, so did hundreds of kids at school.

I looked from the book back to Julie's distraught face. She was still trying to talk, and I said, "Stop crying, slow down, I can't understand what you're saying."

"I know, I know," she mumbled, sniffing and

trying to blink back the tears. I caught ". . . show you . . . " and a few indistinct words as she turned to my desk, pushed aside the homework paper I had been working on, and put down her book. She crushed the pages recklessly as she turned them, searching for the page she wanted. "There, *there!*" She jabbed a finger against a page, and I huddled beside her, our heads over the book, our eyes following the lines of print traced by her finger:

> *Without a tighter breathing,*
> *And zero at the bone.*

My eyes flew to the top of the page, to the poem's title, "A narrow fellow in the grass." I knew this poem. It was about a snake. I shivered. Even the thought of snakes filled me with dread—with the exact sensation the poet had described, cold dread so complete it froze my bones.

"When I read those last lines—" Julie sobbed, covering her face with her hands to shut out whatever it was she was seeing in memory. "It was a snake—he threw a *snake* at me. He called me when I was running in the cemetery. I wanted to go home, I just wanted to go home—it was so dark—Toddy dared us to go—"

"Julie, don't cry. It's okay now. Slow down so I can understand."

But I knew she hadn't even heard me, she was intent on what she wanted to say.

"We were all scattered, and I thought the ghost would get me. I tried to run away so it wouldn't catch me." Her hands were still over her face, and I had to strain to follow what she was saying. "I kept falling over the—over the gravestones and roots of trees. Oh, Allison, I was *so frightened.* You can't imagine—"

"Yes, I can, Julie, honest I can, but it's all right now, you're okay now."

She was out of breath from her torrent of words, and she brushed at her wet cheeks with unsteady fingers. "I didn't know which way to run or how to get out of the cemetery." She was trying to speak more slowly. "I heard someone calling. Someone was calling 'Here, over here!' And then I saw a light. Someone had a candle, and oh, Allison, I was so glad to see the candle, and I ran toward it. But when I got close, I saw Toddy's face in the candlelight, and he was laughing, and he said, '*Ya, ya, ya,*' and he threw—he threw—a *snake* at me. A big—a big—"

Her voice was lost in sobs, and my heart jerked as I put myself there in Julie's place. Coiling through the darkness came the snake, eyes glittering in the last flicker of candlelight before the flame went out . . . and in the darkness a terrified little girl felt the snake slide against her face.

"I was so frightened I couldn't even breathe. I just ran and ran—and then suddenly there wasn't anything under my feet and I began to fall—" Julie tried to control her sobs as she gazed at me with confused, tragic eyes. "There was just no more ground, Allison. There was just no more ground."

"Oh . . . Julie." I felt tears in my own eyes. We stood staring at each other, and below my windows we could hear a car turning into the driveway. My folks were home. Life would continue on its routine course. My desk lamp shone on the open page of the book Julie had brought . . . and on the last lines of Emily Dickinson's poem.

Toddy's snake had probably been dead, but dead or alive the fright and revulsion were the same, and Emily Dickinson had known just how that felt.

> But never met this fellow,
> Attended or alone,
> Without a tighter breathing,
> And zero at the bone.

Chapter Ten

Julie and I went back to the cemetery on Black Hill Road one last time. September was ending and the weather was cool. We walked around in the old section looking for names on markers that were overgrown with tufts of grass; looking for a name we didn't know and never found.

The caretaker was there, clipping a row of bushes in the new section. When we arrived, he gave us a friendly wave. But I think he was curious, too; not many people visited the old section of the cemetery—and we had come twice.

As he went back to his work, two women walked past him toward a grave, heads together as they talked in subdued voices, the whispery voices of churches, libraries, museums, and graveyards. Nearer to us, where the old section and the new section began to blend together, an elderly man stood by a grave with his head bowed in mourning. Birds twittered in the trees, and the September sky, so clear and blue and beautiful, seemed to belong stretched over some more cheerful place.

At the back property line of the cemetery was a fence. Not a fancy, tall iron fence like the one that fronted on Black Hill Road. The back fence was an old chain link fence, rusted in places.

A few feet beyond the fence was the steep drop of a rocky ravine overgrown with trees and scrubby bushes.

"This fence wasn't here then," Julie said, touching the rusted links thoughtfully.

We looked down into the abyss. The drop-off was treacherously abrupt.

"He murdered you, scaring you like that," I said. "Toddy murdered you as surely as if he pushed you down the ravine with his own hands."

Julie was silent.

"I suppose so," she said at last, staring down the rocky ravine where she had died.

"You'd think they would have had *something* here." I pulled on the fence to see how sturdy it was. The fence shuddered as I shook it. "Even *this* isn't great," I said with disgust.

As I drew my hand away a rough place on the fence caught the sleeve of my sweater, as though to get back at me for insulting it.

"If the cemetery always closed at five, nobody

would have been in here after dark—at least not usually."

Julie gave me an ironic glance. "They could get by without a fence," she said. "Look how far we are from the graves. Nobody visiting a grave had any reason to come way back here and fall down into the ravine."

"I suppose you're right," I agreed grudgingly. "And there are a few trees that make kind of a border along the back here. But I still think it was a lousy setup."

A bird called somewhere across the cemetery, and Julie looked up at the sky, letting the wind gently blow the hair across her forehead for a moment before she reached up and brushed it back.

We walked a little way along the fence line, and I stooped to pick up a long twig that had fallen from a nearby tree. I started to drag the stick along the links of the fence, listening to the clicking noise it made— *rat-tat-tat-tat-tat-tat*—a noise broken off abruptly as I felt a hand close roughly on my wrist, yanking my arm away from the fence.

"Don't *do* that!" Julie's voice was filled with anger, a sort of rage that I didn't know better than to run a stick along a fence. As I gaped at her with amazement, she continued to hold my wrist, shaking it as if to shake free the twig I still held. I let the twig drop, and it fell lightly to the weedy patch of grass beside the fence. Slowly Julie released my wrist, and I rubbed the place where she had gripped me.

"Oh, Allison, I'm sorry." As she saw me rubbing

my wrist all anger vanished and Julie was her old self again, my gentle friend. "I hurt you."

"No, it's okay." I shook my head. "But what—what upset you so?"

I thought she would shake her head and say she didn't know, the way she had when we saw the boy running with the stick against the black iron rails at the front of the cemetery. But she didn't. She looked at me intently. "I thought something terrible would happen if you didn't stop. And I could hear people shouting and making a commotion, and we were crying—"

"Who's we?"

"All of us, all the—all the little kids." Her voice was faltering and I could tell that whatever memory had been triggered was fading.

"What happened then?" I tried to get something more from her, but she turned away and stared helplessly at the twig I had dropped. "I just . . . something awful," she said softly. "After remembering about the snake, I didn't think there was anything else to frighten me."

We drew away from the fence, and that was when I suggested that we look around at the old gravestones and see if she recognized any names. But it was a halfhearted project. The caretaker obviously lavished more caretaking on the new section, and the scraggly grass drooping in long, weedy clumps over the markers made reading the names difficult. At one grave a few wildflowers were growing, and I wished the whole place could be wildflowers covering everything, grass, gravestones, everything. Just a sea of wildflowers under the blue of the September sky.

As we made our way toward the gate, the caretaker was nowhere in sight. The two women were still there, but the elderly man was gone. I could see a bunch of white cosmos he had left by the grave; their fragile petals moved gently in the breeze, keeping vigil alone.

"I'm never coming back here," Julie said firmly.

I knew we wouldn't be back, but I felt a sense of something missing, something further to be known that we didn't yet know. I even had a momentary crazy idea to grab up a stick and run it along the fence as we went out the cemetery gate, just to see if I could rouse any more memories for Julie.

CRAZY IDEAS: *Those things I get when I'm frustrated.*

And that was the way I felt as we started back toward the town square: frustrated. Julie had said all the little kids were crying, and I was ready to bet that it had something to do with Toddy. All the little kids were afraid of Toddy. Julie had told me that so many times. I hated Greenbridge Cemetery and Black Hill Road and Toddy, most of all Toddy. I felt rebellious that we couldn't get even with him somehow, and I made up my mind to tell Julie my last, crazy, far-out idea. It was a million-to-one chance maybe, but I wanted us to try.

"Julie, do you remember that day my mother and her friend came to Greenbridge to shop?"

I tried to keep the rebellion and frustration out of my voice. I tried to sound as if I was making a casual suggestion, and hoped that Julie would give a casual agreement (to a wild idea).

"I remember." Julie nodded absently. The grave-yard was behind us and we would never be back again. Ahead, the September light lay along Black Hill Road, soft and clear and golden. Traffic was leisurely, and we walked along the sidewalk, shuffling through fallen leaves.

"My mom bought a candy dish that day. I just happened to see that it came from a shop owned by somebody named T. Rendley." I looked sideways at Julie. "Does that name sound familiar to you?"

"Rendley?" Julie frowned. "No, I don't think I've ever heard that name."

I waited a moment before saying anything more. We walked on. Then I said, "Maybe you just don't remember it. Maybe that T. could stand for Tod or Toddy."

Julie actually laughed. "Allison, for heaven's sake! T. could stand for a hundred names. Tom, Tim—"

"That's not exactly a hundred," I said.

"Terry, Ted," Julie went on.

"Okay," I agreed. "And it could be a woman, couldn't it? Teresa, Tanya, Tina, Tillie."

"That's right," Julie said. "It could be a woman."

"Or it could be Toddy. Mom said a real old couple owned the shop. Toddy would be real old now, if he's still alive."

Julie stopped walking and faced me. Cars went by on Black Hill Road. Just ahead I could see the sign over the door of Candlewick. Inside I knew the candles were glowing and glimmering like a fairyland.

"What are you getting at?" Julie's tone was suspicious.

"Can we at least go there and see?" I said.

"Go where?"

"T. Rendley. Antiques—Handcrafts—Fine China." I recited what I had memorized from the lid of the cardboard box. "Come on, Julie," I coaxed. "We've come this far, let's not stop now. Let's at least go to that shop and see if you recognize anybody there."

"How can I recognize anybody after all these years?" Julie objected. She started to walk on, shaking her head. "Everybody's dead that I ever knew," she said. "Or if they're not dead, they'd be real, real old by now. They wouldn't look anything like I remember them."

I knew she was right. It made sense. But I still wanted to go. I still wanted to see T. Rendley at Antiques—Handcrafts—Fine China.

We had to ask the way. None of the shops around the square was T. Rendley's. We got directions to cross the square and go half a block down Holbrook Street.

"Now that's not so far," I encouraged Julie.

She still looked uncertain about going, but she didn't say anything.

In the square, the fountain with the stone fish

was silent, turned off now that summer was over. A few autumn leaves floated in a shallow layer of rainwater in the fountain's basin.

Holbrook Street was a narrow, cobbled street with its share of shoppers and antique hunters. I walked a little ahead of Julie, keeping a lookout for T. Rendley. When I spotted the sign, it was over the doorway of a shop on the opposite side of the street.

"There it is." I stopped so suddenly that Julie bumped into me. "There—across the street."

We stood and looked at the shop. It was very much like the other shops, quaint leaded windows displaying gift items and antiques. The sign bore the same information that had been printed on the cardboard box:

T. RENDLEY
ANTIQUES HANDCRAFTS
FINE CHINA

"Shall we go across—" I started to say, when the door of the shop opened and an old man came out and lounged against the side of the shop by the door. He lit up a pipe, squinting as the smoke drifted across his face.

"The missus still won't let you smoke inside?" A passerby greeted the old man with a chuckle. The old man muttered something I couldn't make out. He didn't seem as amused about the situation as his friend did. When the passerby went on, the man was still muttering to himself.

"Could that be Toddy?" I whispered to Julie as we hung back on our side of the street. "He's awfully old. He could be about the right age."

There was no answer.

"Julie?" I turned to look at her. She had the same strange, almost hypnotized look on her face that she had had the day we went into Martha-Ann Gifts and she recognized the rooms in the back, the same look she had had when we first came to the cemetery at the end of Black Hill Road.

"Julie?" I said again.

She was staring at the old man so intently I thought he would look up at any moment and yell, "What do you two think you're looking at?" He looked crabby enough to do something like that.

But he wasn't paying any attention to us. He lounged against the shop by the doorway, puffing on his pipe and looking cross. He was hatless, and thin wisps of white hair lifted a little in the light breeze that found its way along Holbrook Street.

"I remember now why nobody was allowed to scold Toddy," Julie said, and just as she started to speak I noticed that the hand with which the man held his pipe had only two fingers.

"He was hurt out on the farm." Julie's voice sounded strange. She turned and pretended to be looking at the shop window we were standing next to.

"How? What happened?" I urged her, but she didn't really answer me. She was simply remembering.

"All the grownups said we should be especially kind to him, even when he wasn't being good. We mustn't scold poor Toddy, my mother always said. Poor Toddy—that's what they called him after the accident, at least all that summer after the accident."

And of course Julie hadn't lived to know anything past that summer.

"Then that's really *him*?" I gazed at Julie with awe. Our quest had revealed all the things I had hardly dared hope for.

Julie was pale. "It *must* be him, Allison."

I pretended to look in the shop window too, so the old man wouldn't see me staring at him.

"Is he looking at us?" Julie sounded fearful. "Does he see us?"

I peeked over my shoulder. The old man was not even looking in our direction.

"What if he does see us?" I reminded Julie. "He certainly won't know who you are."

"I know, I know," Julie brushed aside this logic, "I just don't want him to see me."

"Aren't we going over?" I felt impatient with Julie. I wanted to talk to this man, and she was afraid he would see us.

I looked across the street again. Now the old man was knocking ash from his pipe. He opened his shop door and went inside. Light reflecting on the shop window hid everyone inside from view, and the old man had disappeared into this place where we could no longer see him.

"He's gone," I said, and Julie looked around cautiously to be sure I was right.

"Were you there when the accident happened? Were you at the farm that day?"

"No, I wasn't," Julie shook her head. "Please, Allison, let's go before he comes back out."

"Before he comes back out? I want to go into the shop. Don't you want to talk to him?"

Julie looked startled. "Oh, *no*, Allison. What would I say to him?"

"I don't know exactly," I admitted, "but it seems as if you ought to do something to pay him back for what he did, even if it's just scaring him out of his wits by telling him who you used to be, that you've come back to life."

Julie drew away from me. "No, I don't want to talk to him. Let's just *go*."

She was just as afraid of Toddy now as she had been when she was a little girl. She was afraid of spiders in a teacup and whatever else Toddy might do next. Afraid of him on cobbled streets and snowy sledding hills. She was afraid the bird would fly in the door and peck out her eyes. And she was still seeing Toddy's face in the candlelight, still hearing his voice, "*Ya, ya, ya,*" as the snake came writhing toward her through the air.

"You're afraid," I said accusingly. "How can you be afraid of him *now*? What happened was years and years and years ago. He can't hurt you now. But you ought to get even somehow."

"No, no, no."

"You ought to pay him back—"

She cut me off by turning and walking away.

I stood by myself for a moment, and then I hurried along the sidewalk and caught up with Julie.

"Hey, it's okay," I said, falling into step beside her. "If you don't want to talk to him, you don't want to talk to him."

We had reached the square, and Julie sank down on one of the benches shaded by maple trees.

"Oh, I *was* there, Allison," she blurted out to my complete surprise. "I lied to you. I *was* there."

"At the farm? When the accident happened?"

"Yes." She nodded miserably. "We were playing by the pump—we weren't supposed to be, though. We weren't supposed to go near the pump jack."

"What's the pump jack?"

Julie didn't seem to hear me. Memories were coming strong and clear.

"The little kids were supposed to stay away from the horse stalls, and not go up the ladder in the hayloft, and not play around the pump jack when it was working. There was a big metal gear that went around—and Toddy stuck long blades of grass in the gear wheel to see them get chopped up. We were all clustered around watching, and then I said, 'Try a stick, Toddy.' I picked up the first stick I saw and someone said, 'That's too short,' but I gave it to Toddy anyway, and he stuck the stick into the gears, and it went tapping along, tap-tap-tap-tap, and then—it all happened so fast—somehow his fingers were in the gears."

I felt an involuntary shudder sweep along my body. "Oh, Julie. . . ."

"And then everyone was shouting and running, and I was crying . . . oh, Allison, it was my fault, it was my *fault*."

Julie looked at me with an expression of anguish. I had a blurry, confused vision of old-fashioned farm equipment I didn't know anything about; running, shouting, crying little children streaking for help toward a farmhouse that must have seemed a long way off; a terribly hurt boy . . . but I forced myself to think of Julie.

"It *wasn't* your fault!" I caught her arm and gave it a shake. "Toddy was showing off to be fooling around with that pump whatever-it-was in the first place."

"Pump jack," Julie said. "It was for pumping water to the barn animals."

That still didn't mean a lot to me, but I got the idea: it was a piece of farm machinery the children were supposed to stay away from, and Toddy knew better than to be sticking things in the gears, especially a short stick that would suck his fingers in.

"Julie, it *wasn't* your *fault*," I said again.

"Toddy thought it was," Julie said sadly. "He hated me. He threw the snake at me on purpose that night, Allison. It wasn't just by chance that I was the one. It wasn't just by chance."

Chapter Eleven

When Julie and I left Greenbridge, we left a long-ago time to return to our present lives and a modern world . . . where what we had done, what we had found out, would not be believed or understood by most people.

If we had told them.

But we haven't told anyone.

Greenbridge, the shops around the square, the silent fountain with two stone fish, are permanent pictures in my mind—in a gallery that also holds pictures of gravestones and the iron gate of a ceme-tery, a little girl playing a music box, and an old man smoking a pipe beside a shop doorway on a narrow, cobbled street.

The autumn days are passing. The trees are bare

now, and sometimes on the way to school I see a few small, sparse snowflakes whirling in the wind, the first scant flakes of winter, November snow.

The days are colorless. The light in November is like no other light of any other time of year. It is an ominous light, I think, bleak and filled with loneliness. The afternoons are short. Winter is coming; it is in the wind, like the snowflakes and the cold.

Always at this time of year, in the bleak, cold days of November, my own special memories grow stronger. Faces, voices, sounds in rooms I once knew, hovering at the edge of my mind like Julie's memories, press in upon me more intensely, and I am aware of fear. I seem to know that something to be greatly feared happened to me once, at just this time of year, on just such a November day as the ones unfolding now.

When Julie told me how she remembered things from a former life, the tune on the music box, the spider in the teacup, I wanted to cry out, "Yes, yes, yes, I know what you mean!" Because memories whisper to me, too, and nag at my mind. Julie was so happy that I understood her and that I didn't laugh at her. Oh, it was so easy for me to understand. I wanted to say, "Me, too, Julie, me, too."

But I was afraid she might think I was making fun of her, and then she would stop telling me the things she remembered. And I wanted to hear everything she had to say, so I kept quiet about myself.

Before that afternoon when I heard Julie playing "Three Blind Mice," before our trips to Greenbridge, I used to think it was useless, that I could never actually track back my own former life. But now I know I can. Julie found her former life, or at least enough fragments to form an idea of the whole. Doors opened magically. And they will open for me. I will find my life the way Julie found hers. I will find my life . . . and my death.

Someday I will be someplace and I will *know* that it is the place where I lived, the way Julie knew that afternoon with her mother in Greenbridge. There will be a church bell ringing, for I hear that often in my memories. The sound of the bell comes distantly, as though from the far end of whatever town I lived in.

And somewhere in this place I will find a room with a long, dark, polished table glimmering in the faint evening light. Reflections will move across the surface of the table like underwater creatures swimming upward toward the dusky light of the room. There will be an echo of laughter in my memories of this room with the beautiful table, and I think I was very happy there.

There are other happy memories—a bird singing in a cage . . . a small pearl ring on a hand reaching gently toward me . . . a field of wildflowers under the blue of the sky.

But there is also a street on a cold gray day. I hear the sound of footsteps coming toward me as I crouch against the rough stone wall of some house along the street, my heart pounding with terror. Terror of what? Of whom?

Someday I will know.

The footsteps come toward me rapidly and stop as the shadow of my pursuer falls over me. I open my mouth to scream, but I can't. My body is paralyzed with fear and my scream is frozen in my throat, like the silent scream in a nightmare.

Was I murdered like Julie? I look from school windows as the dark November days pass one by one, and the first snowflakes fall. Whatever it was, *beware*! Whoever harmed me, *beware*! I will find you, and I will not be afraid as Julie was. I will find you, and I will make you sorry for what you did. I will not turn away the way Julie turned away on Holbrook Street.

Whoever you are, I will find you and have my revenge.

BEWARE: A *word of warning spoken by me* *this day.*

ABOUT THE AUTHOR

CAROL BEACH YORK is a writer with over forty outstanding juvenile and young adult books to her credit, including the popular Bantam titles *Remember Me When I Am Dead*, *I Will Make You Disappear*, *Miss Know It All*, and *Miss Know It All Returns*. Born and raised in Chicago, she began her career writing short stories and sold her first one to *Seventeen* magazine. Her first teen novel, a romance, *Sparrow Lake*, was published in 1962. Since then she has contributed many stories and articles to magazines in both the juvenile and adult markets, in addition to her activity as a novelist. She especially enjoys writing suspense stories. Ms. York lives in Chicago with her daughter, Diana.